The STAR of MELVIN

The **STAR** *of*
MELVIN

by
NATHAN ZIMELMAN

illustrated by
OLIVIER DUNREA

Macmillan Publishing Company   New York

Collier Macmillan Publishers   London

Macmillan Publishing Company, 866 Third Avenue, New York, NY 10022
Collier Macmillan Canada, Inc.
Printed and bound by South China Printing Company, Hong Kong
First American Edition

10 9 8 7 6 5 4 3 2 1

The text of this book is set in 14 point Galliard.
The illustrations are rendered in gouache and colored pencil.
Library of Congress Cataloging-in-Publication Data
Zimelman, Nathan. The star of Melvin.
Summary: Melvin the angel, a newly appointed star
polisher, shines his small star to such perfection
that God chooses it to become the Star of Bethlehem.
[1. Angels – Fiction. 2. Stars – Fiction]
I. Dunrea, Olivier, ill. II. Title.
PZ7.Z57St 1987 [E] 86-171
ISBN 0-02-793750-X

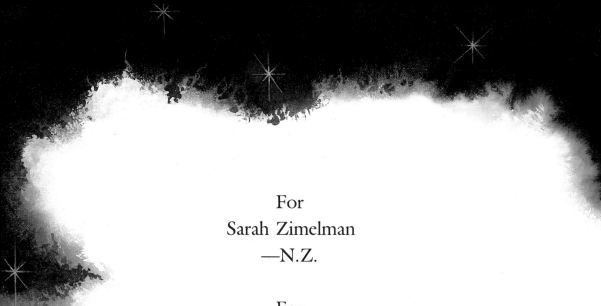

For
Sarah Zimelman
—N.Z.

For
Barbara Wexler
and
Philip Lee
—O.D.

Melvin was an angel.

He was not a very important angel.
He did not sit at the right hand of God.
He did not sit at the left hand of God.
When all the angels assembled and sat to hear the
wisdom of God, Melvin stood.
Melvin stood, holding a broom and a box, waiting.

And when Melvin saw any litter, he would rush over
and sweep it into his box.
It wasn't much of a job. Angels were so very clean.
Maybe once in a thousand years, a tiny feather would
flutter down to be pounced on and swept up by Melvin.

What Melvin really wanted was to be a cloud sweeper.
Or, best of bests, a star shiner.
Whenever a job opening was posted on the heavenly
bulletin board, Melvin was first in line.

But when he was given a cloud broom and told to sweep, the broom was so large and Melvin so small that the broom swept Melvin.

As for the polishing cloth of a star shiner, Melvin could barely lift it, and when he did, it exploded out of his hands and swallowed him in its soft, soft folds.

Melvin didn't stop trying, though. And one day, to his astonishment, he was not only first in line, he was the whole of the line.

"Am I too early?" Melvin asked the Angel-in-Charge. The Angel-in-Charge did not look up from the large ledger his quill pen was hurrying across. "No."

"Am I too late?"
  The Angel-in-Charge crossed a *t* and dotted an *i*.
"You are just in time."

He held out a polishing cloth.

"Go ten million miles to the west and take one step left
and you will find the star you have been assigned."

Melvin couldn't believe his ears.

He had been made a star shiner.

He couldn't believe his eyes, either.

The polishing cloth fitted his hands perfectly.

"It's a very small star," said the Angel-in-Charge.

"Do you want the job?"

"I do! I do!" cried Melvin.

"Good. Because nobody else does."

It really wasn't the sort of star most star shiners would like. It was so very small. And it was dull. There was hardly a glimmer to it.
But it was all that Melvin had ever wanted.

He polished his star morning and noon. And far into the evening, when the other star shiners had put aside their polishing cloths, Melvin would still be polishing away.

Even when Melvin was going home, he never left all at once. He would always come back to give his star one more rub with the sleeve of his robe.

Slowly, not in a day, or a year, or two thousand years,
Melvin's dull star began to shine.
The heavens around it that had been dark and
foreboding grew brighter and happier.

Melvin's days were so joyously busy that if his friend
Gamaliel had not come visiting, he never would have
heard of the competition.

But Gamaliel did come visiting, and when he saw
Melvin's star sparkling away, he said, "You should enter
your star in the star contest, Melvin."
Melvin looked at his star. "It's kind of small for a contest."
Gamaliel said, "Nothing was said about large, Melvin.
This is a very bright and very cheery star."
"It is," Melvin agreed.

This time Melvin wasn't first in line. In fact, he was last.
In front of him stood huge angel after huge angel star
shiner, each one holding a gigantic, fiercely glittering star.

Gamaliel nudged Melvin. "Maybe this wasn't such a good idea, after all."

"Big isn't everything," Melvin said, giving his star another rub.

The line moved slowly past God.
As each magnificently fiery star was presented to him,
God would shake his head and say, "No, no. It's not
right for a birth day."

At last only Melvin was left.

But just as Melvin was about to stand before God with
his star, a trumpet call sounded. Heaven trembled, and
the angels threw up their hands in despair.
The Archangel Gabriel had come to enter the contest.
And the Archangel Gabriel never lost.

With a great golden trumpet in his right hand and a
tremendous star held high in his left, Gabriel stalked
down the aisle of angels.

He presented his star to God. The star twirled and
sparkled with every color that ever had been or would be.
Then Gabriel stepped back, waiting to be proclaimed
the winner.

But God, who sees everything, saw Melvin still waiting.
"The contest is not yet over," he said. "Come, Melvin.
Show me your star."

Melvin stepped forward and held up his star for God.

God looked down at the gently shining star, and nodded his head. He smiled. "Melvin, you understood," God said. "This is the right star."

All the angels in heaven cheered, and Gabriel blew
a note on his golden trumpet.
"Now, Melvin," said God, "come with me."

Holding his star, Melvin followed as God walked
across the heavens.

Every so often God looked back at the cheery light of
Melvin's star. "He'll like it," God said. "Yes, he'll like it."

At last, God stopped at a dark and empty space.
"Place it here, Melvin. So, so, just so.

"How nicely it fits," God said. "How its light gladdens
what it shines upon. Look, Melvin, look."

Melvin gave his star one last rub with the sleeve
of his robe.
Then, as the star shone brighter and brighter, Melvin
looked ... down upon the town of Bethlehem.